THE WONDERFUL WIZARD OF OZ

VOL. 7

ADAPTED FROM THE NOVEL BY L. FRANK BAUM

Writer: ERIC SHANOWER
Artist: SKOTTIE YOUNG
Colorist: JEAN-FRANCOIS BEAULIEU
Letterer: JEFF ECKLEBERRY

Assistant Editors: LAUREN SANKOVITCH & LAUREN HENRY
Associate Editor: NATE COSBY
Senior Editor: RALPH MACCHIO

Special Thanks to Chris Allo, Rich Ginter, Jeff Suter & Jim Nausedas
Collection Editor: MARK D. BEAZLEY
Assistant Editors: NELSON RIBEIRO & ALEX STARBUCK
Editor, Special Projects: JENNIFER GRÜNWALD
Senior Editor, Special Projects: JEFF YOUNGQUIST
SVP of Print & Digital Publishing Sales: DAVID GABRIEL
Production: JERRY KALINOWSKI
Book Design: SPRING HOTELING

Editor in Chief: AXEL ALONSO
Chief Creative Officer: JOE QUESADA
Publisher: DAN BUCKLEY
Executive Producer: ALAN FINE

visit us at www.abdopublishing.com

Reinforced library bound edition published in 2014 by Spotlight, a division of the ABDO Group, PO Box 398166, Minneapolis, Minnesota 55439. Spotlight produces high-quality reinforced library bound editions for schools and libraries. Published by agreement with Marvel Characters, Inc.

Printed in the United States of America, North Mankato, Minnesota.
102013
012014
This book contains at least 10% recycled materials.

MARVEL
Marvel.com

Library of Congress Cataloging-in-Publication Data

Shanower, Eric.
The wonderful Wizard of Oz / adapted from the novel by L. Frank Baum ; writer: Eric Shanower ; artist: Skottie Young. -- Reinforced library bound edition.
pages cm
"Marvel."
Summary: An eight-volume, graphic novel adaptation of L. Frank Baum's tales of Dorothy, a little girl from Kansas who is blown by a storm to the magical land of Oz, where she has amazing adventures while trying to get home.
ISBN 978-1-61479-226-0 (vol. 1) -- ISBN 978-1-61479-227-7 (vol. 2) -- ISBN 978-1-61479-228-4 (vol. 3) -- ISBN 978-1-61479-229-1 (vol. 4) -- ISBN 978-1-61479-230-7 (vol. 5) -- ISBN 978-1-61479-231-4 (vol. 6) -- ISBN 978-1-61479-232-1 (vol. 7) -- ISBN 978-1-61479-233-8 (vol. 8)
1. Graphic novels. [1. Graphic novels. 2. Fantasy.] I. Young, Skottie, illustrator. II. Baum, L. Frank (Lyman Frank), 1856-1919. III. Title.
PZ7.7.S453Won 2014
741.5'973--dc23

2013029128

Spotlight

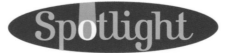

All Spotlight books are reinforced library binding and manufactured in the United States of America.

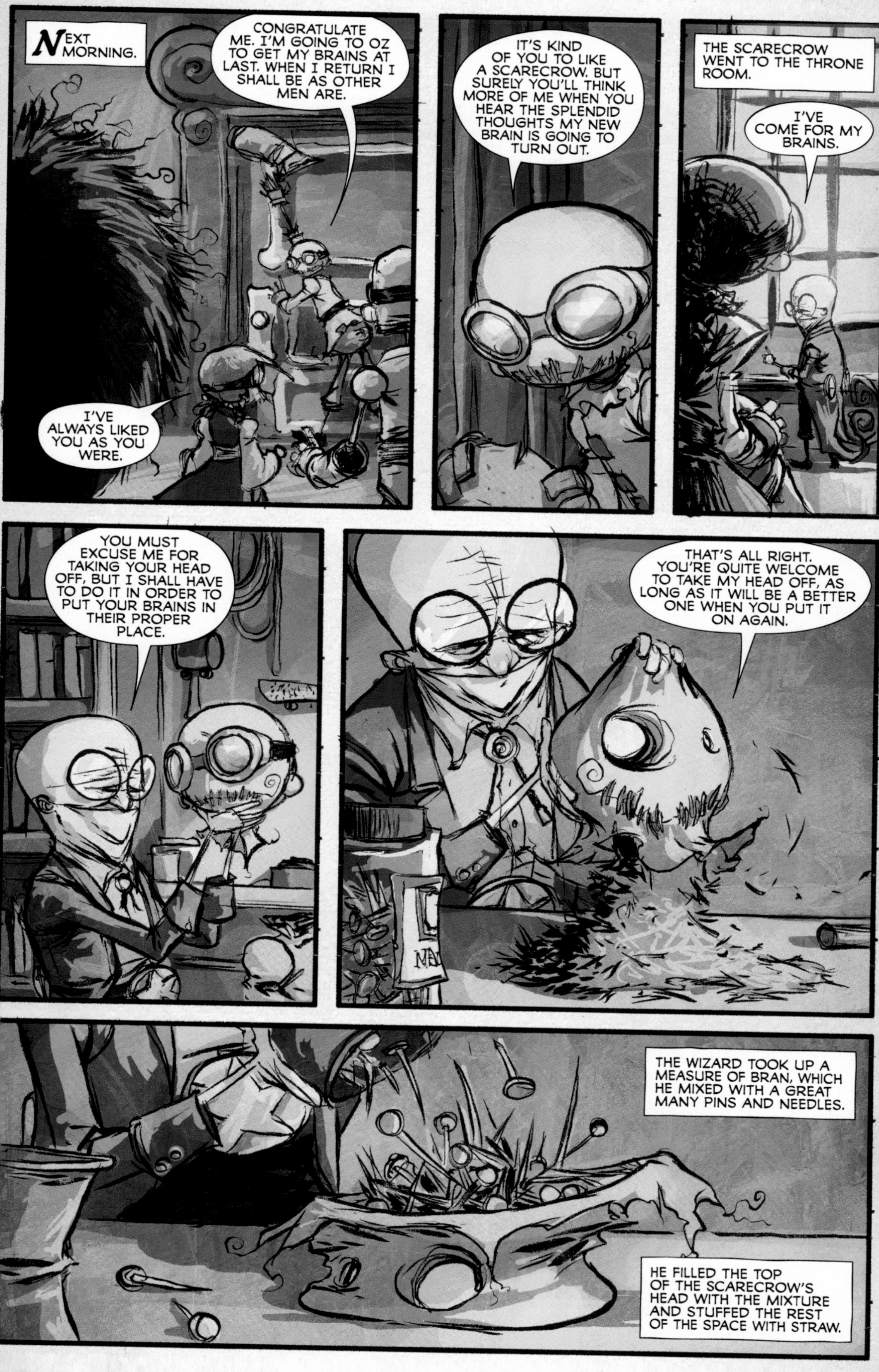

NEXT MORNING.
CONGRATULATE ME. I'M GOING TO OZ TO GET MY BRAINS AT LAST. WHEN I RETURN I SHALL BE AS OTHER MEN ARE.
I'VE ALWAYS LIKED YOU AS YOU WERE.
IT'S KIND OF YOU TO LIKE A SCARECROW. BUT SURELY YOU'LL THINK MORE OF ME WHEN YOU HEAR THE SPLENDID THOUGHTS MY NEW BRAIN IS GOING TO TURN OUT.
THE SCARECROW WENT TO THE THRONE ROOM.
I'VE COME FOR MY BRAINS.
YOU MUST EXCUSE ME FOR TAKING YOUR HEAD OFF, BUT I SHALL HAVE TO DO IT IN ORDER TO PUT YOUR BRAINS IN THEIR PROPER PLACE.
THAT'S ALL RIGHT. YOU'RE QUITE WELCOME TO TAKE MY HEAD OFF, AS LONG AS IT WILL BE A BETTER ONE WHEN YOU PUT IT ON AGAIN.
THE WIZARD TOOK UP A MEASURE OF BRAN, WHICH HE MIXED WITH A GREAT MANY PINS AND NEEDLES.
HE FILLED THE TOP OF THE SCARECROW'S HEAD WITH THE MIXTURE AND STUFFED THE REST OF THE SPACE WITH STRAW.

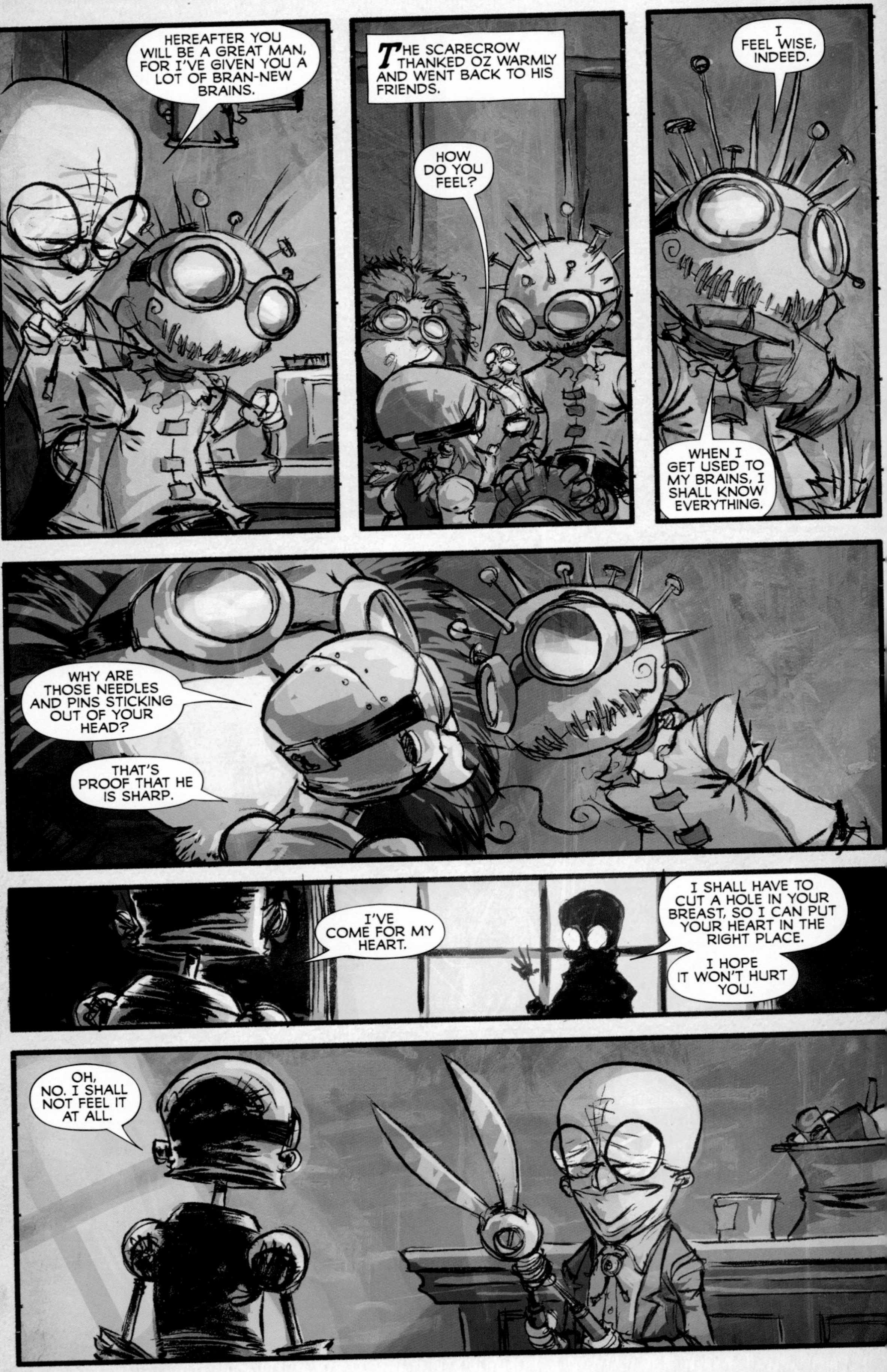
HEREAFTER YOU WILL BE A GREAT MAN, FOR I'VE GIVEN YOU A LOT OF BRAN-NEW BRAINS.
THE SCARECROW THANKED OZ WARMLY AND WENT BACK TO HIS FRIENDS.
HOW DO YOU FEEL?
I FEEL WISE, INDEED.
WHEN I GET USED TO MY BRAINS, I SHALL KNOW EVERYTHING.
WHY ARE THOSE NEEDLES AND PINS STICKING OUT OF YOUR HEAD?
THAT'S PROOF THAT HE IS SHARP.
I'VE COME FOR MY HEART.
I SHALL HAVE TO CUT A HOLE IN YOUR BREAST, SO I CAN PUT YOUR HEART IN THE RIGHT PLACE.
I HOPE IT WON'T HURT YOU.
OH, NO. I SHALL NOT FEEL IT AT ALL.

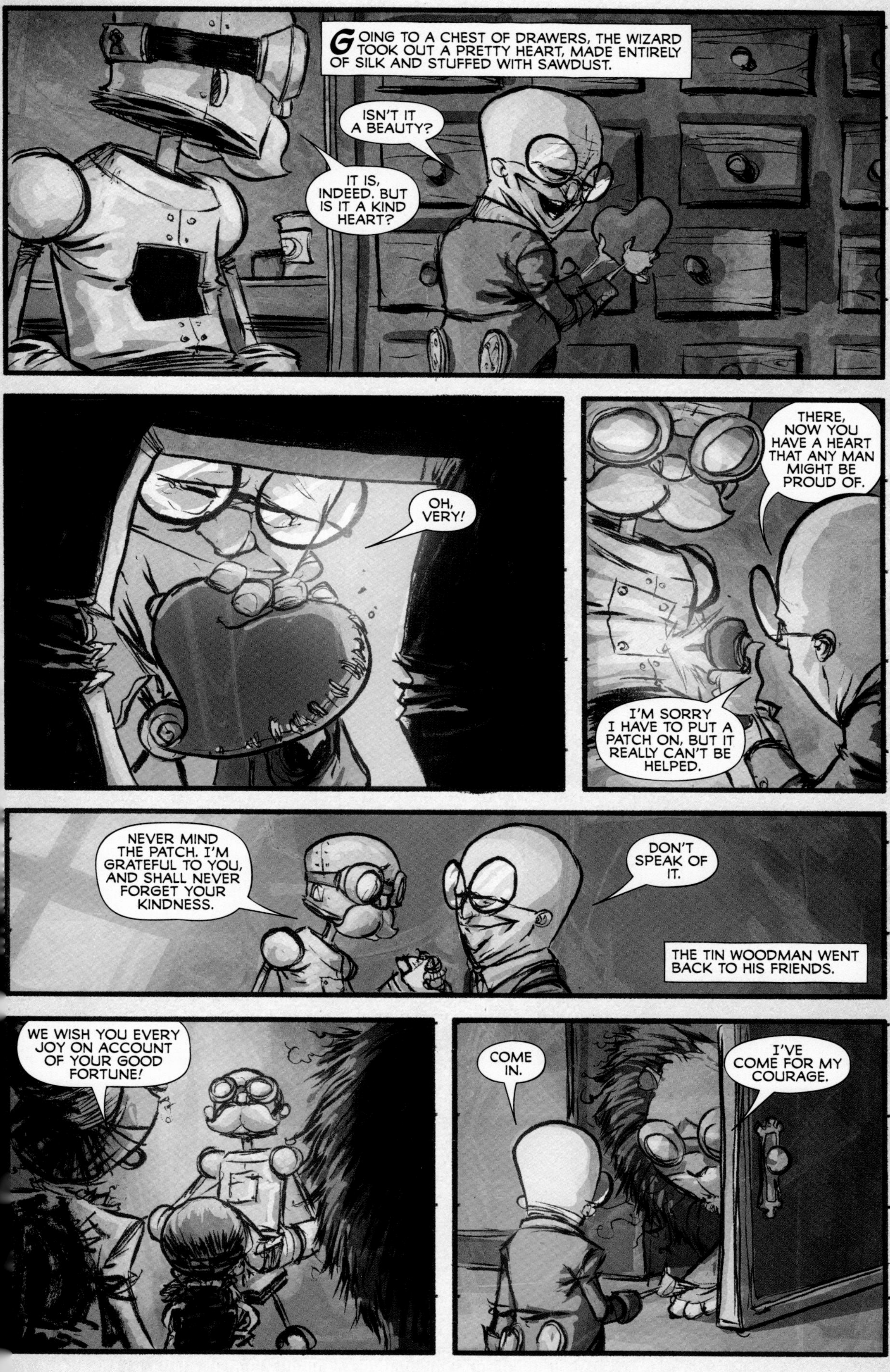
GOING TO A CHEST OF DRAWERS, THE WIZARD TOOK OUT A PRETTY HEART, MADE ENTIRELY OF SILK AND STUFFED WITH SAWDUST.
ISN'T IT A BEAUTY?
IT IS, INDEED. BUT IS IT A KIND HEART?
OH, VERY!
THERE, NOW YOU HAVE A HEART THAT ANY MAN MIGHT BE PROUD OF.
I'M SORRY I HAVE TO PUT A PATCH ON, BUT IT REALLY CAN'T BE HELPED.
NEVER MIND THE PATCH. I'M GRATEFUL TO YOU, AND SHALL NEVER FORGET YOUR KINDNESS.
DON'T SPEAK OF IT.
THE TIN WOODMAN WENT BACK TO HIS FRIENDS.
WE WISH YOU EVERY JOY ON ACCOUNT OF YOUR GOOD FORTUNE!
COME IN.
I'VE COME FOR MY COURAGE.

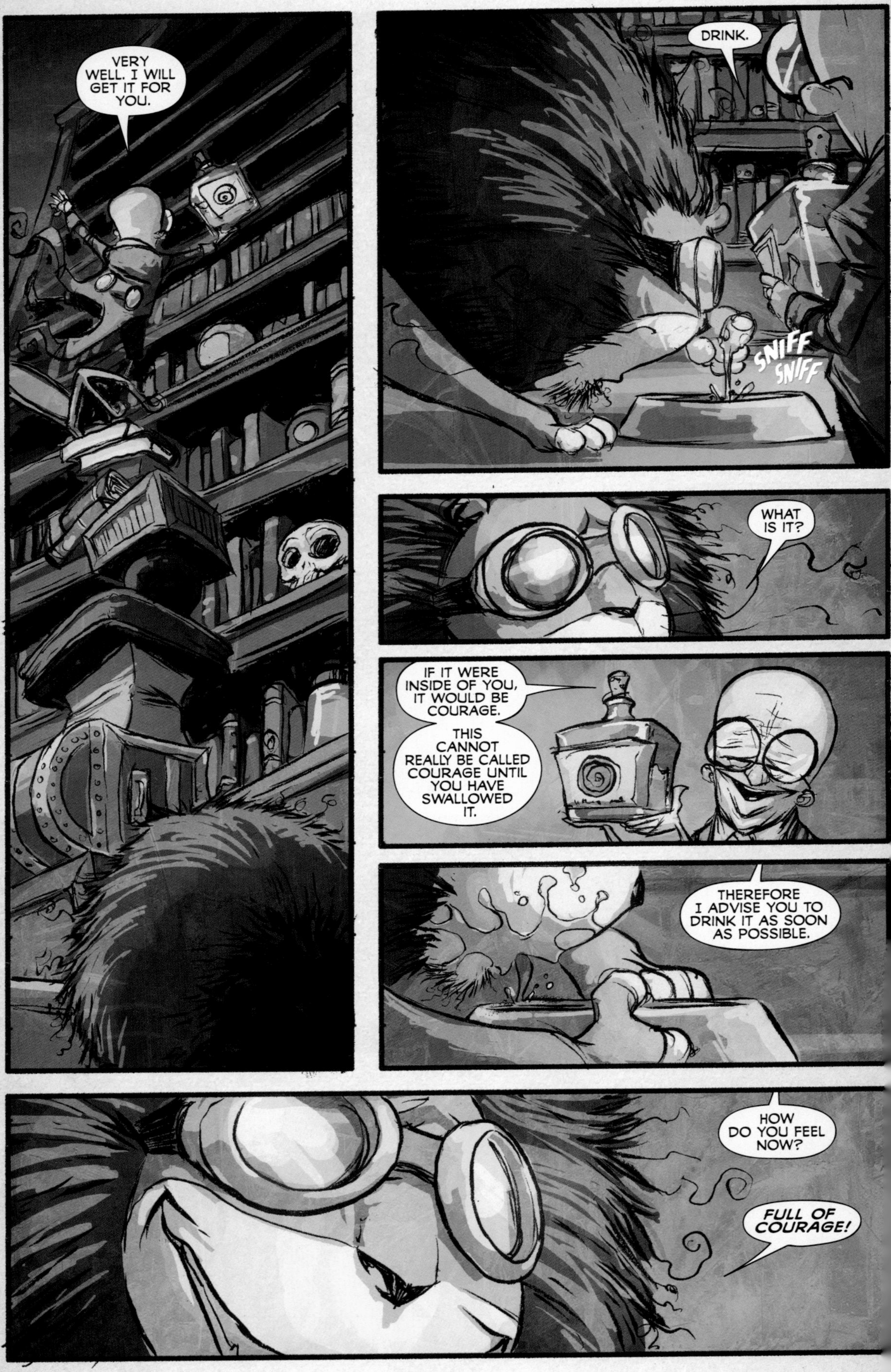
VERY WELL. I WILL GET IT FOR YOU.
DRINK.
SNIFF SNIFF
WHAT IS IT?
IF IT WERE INSIDE OF YOU, IT WOULD BE COURAGE.
THIS CANNOT REALLY BE CALLED COURAGE UNTIL YOU HAVE SWALLOWED IT.
THEREFORE I ADVISE YOU TO DRINK IT AS SOON AS POSSIBLE.
HOW DO YOU FEEL NOW?
FULL OF COURAGE!

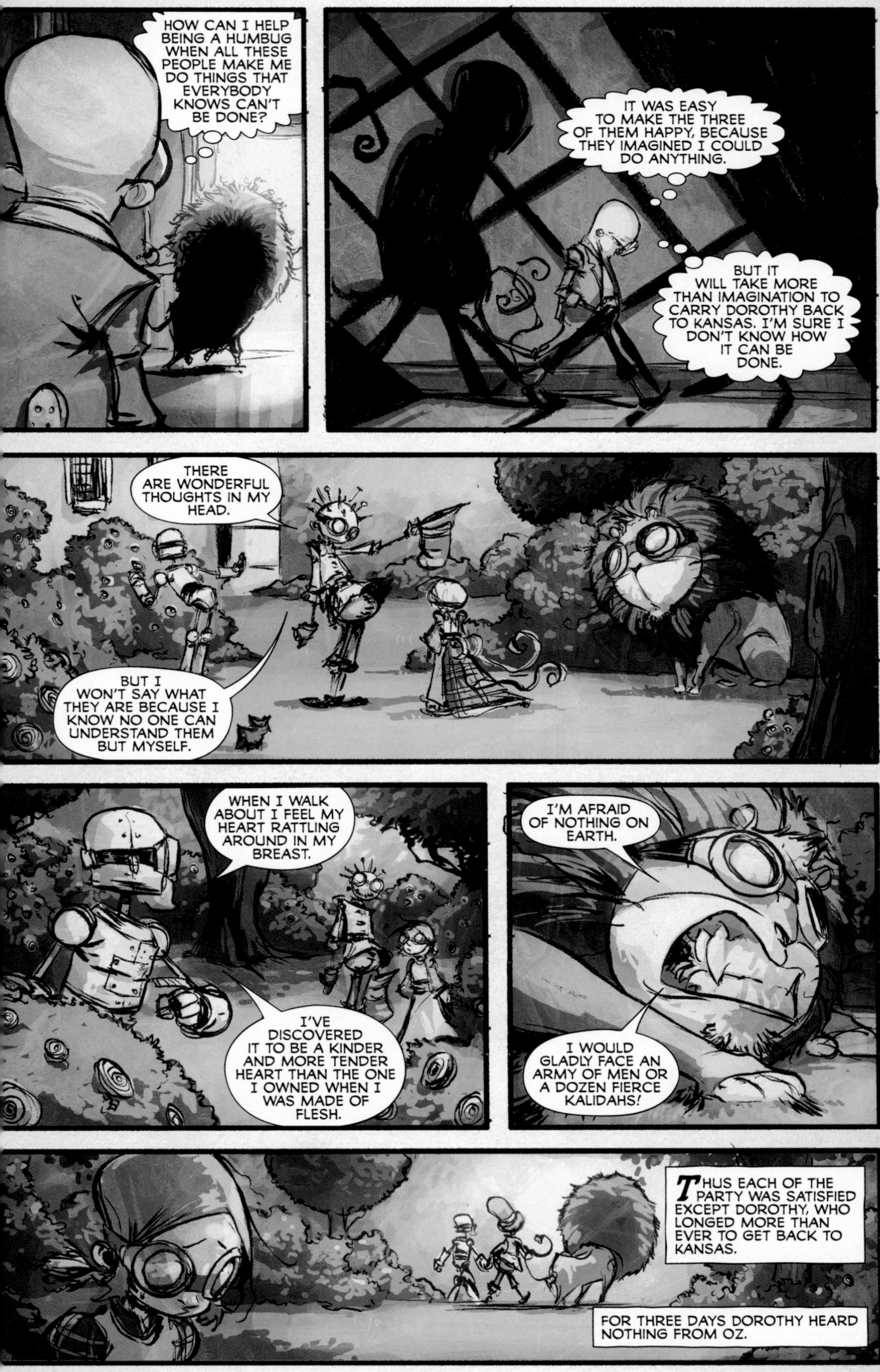
HOW CAN I HELP BEING A HUMBUG WHEN ALL THESE PEOPLE MAKE ME DO THINGS THAT EVERYBODY KNOWS CAN'T BE DONE?
IT WAS EASY TO MAKE THE THREE OF THEM HAPPY, BECAUSE THEY IMAGINED I COULD DO ANYTHING.
BUT IT WILL TAKE MORE THAN IMAGINATION TO CARRY DOROTHY BACK TO KANSAS. I'M SURE I DON'T KNOW HOW IT CAN BE DONE.
THERE ARE WONDERFUL THOUGHTS IN MY HEAD.
BUT I WON'T SAY WHAT THEY ARE BECAUSE I KNOW NO ONE CAN UNDERSTAND THEM BUT MYSELF.
WHEN I WALK ABOUT I FEEL MY HEART RATTLING AROUND IN MY BREAST.
I'VE DISCOVERED IT TO BE A KINDER AND MORE TENDER HEART THAN THE ONE I OWNED WHEN I WAS MADE OF FLESH.
I'M AFRAID OF NOTHING ON EARTH.
I WOULD GLADLY FACE AN ARMY OF MEN OR A DOZEN FIERCE KALIDAHS!
THUS EACH OF THE PARTY WAS SATISFIED EXCEPT DOROTHY, WHO LONGED MORE THAN EVER TO GET BACK TO KANSAS.
FOR THREE DAYS DOROTHY HEARD NOTHING FROM OZ.

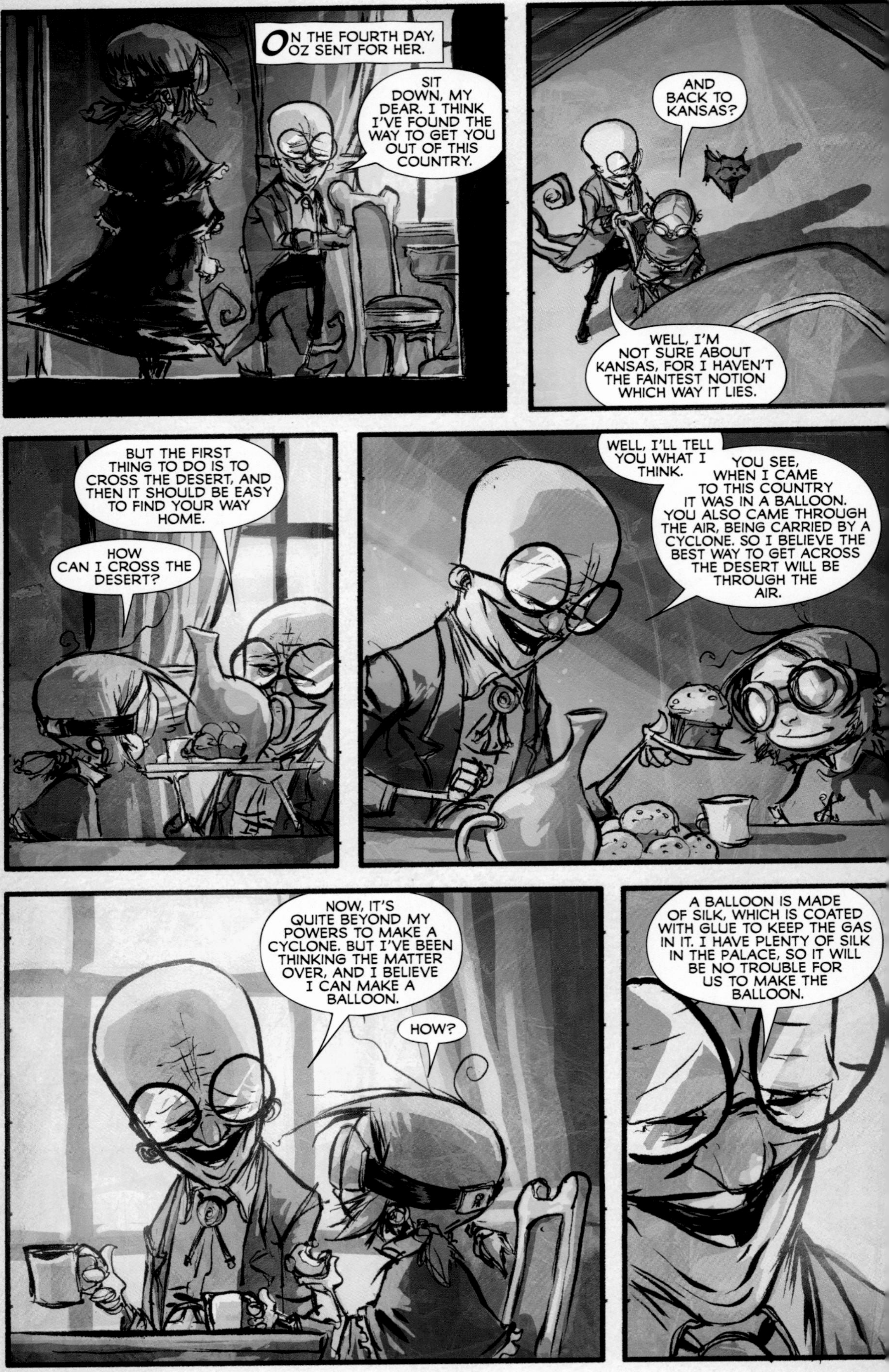
ON THE FOURTH DAY, OZ SENT FOR HER.
SIT DOWN, MY DEAR. I THINK I'VE FOUND THE WAY TO GET YOU OUT OF THIS COUNTRY.
AND BACK TO KANSAS?
WELL, I'M NOT SURE ABOUT KANSAS, FOR I HAVEN'T THE FAINTEST NOTION WHICH WAY IT LIES.
BUT THE FIRST THING TO DO IS TO CROSS THE DESERT, AND THEN IT SHOULD BE EASY TO FIND YOUR WAY HOME.
HOW CAN I CROSS THE DESERT?
WELL, I'LL TELL YOU WHAT I THINK.
YOU SEE, WHEN I CAME TO THIS COUNTRY IT WAS IN A BALLOON. YOU ALSO CAME THROUGH THE AIR, BEING CARRIED BY A CYCLONE. SO I BELIEVE THE BEST WAY TO GET ACROSS THE DESERT WILL BE THROUGH THE AIR.
NOW, IT'S QUITE BEYOND MY POWERS TO MAKE A CYCLONE. BUT I'VE BEEN THINKING THE MATTER OVER, AND I BELIEVE I CAN MAKE A BALLOON.
HOW?
A BALLOON IS MADE OF SILK, WHICH IS COATED WITH GLUE TO KEEP THE GAS IN IT. I HAVE PLENTY OF SILK IN THE PALACE, SO IT WILL BE NO TROUBLE FOR US TO MAKE THE BALLOON.

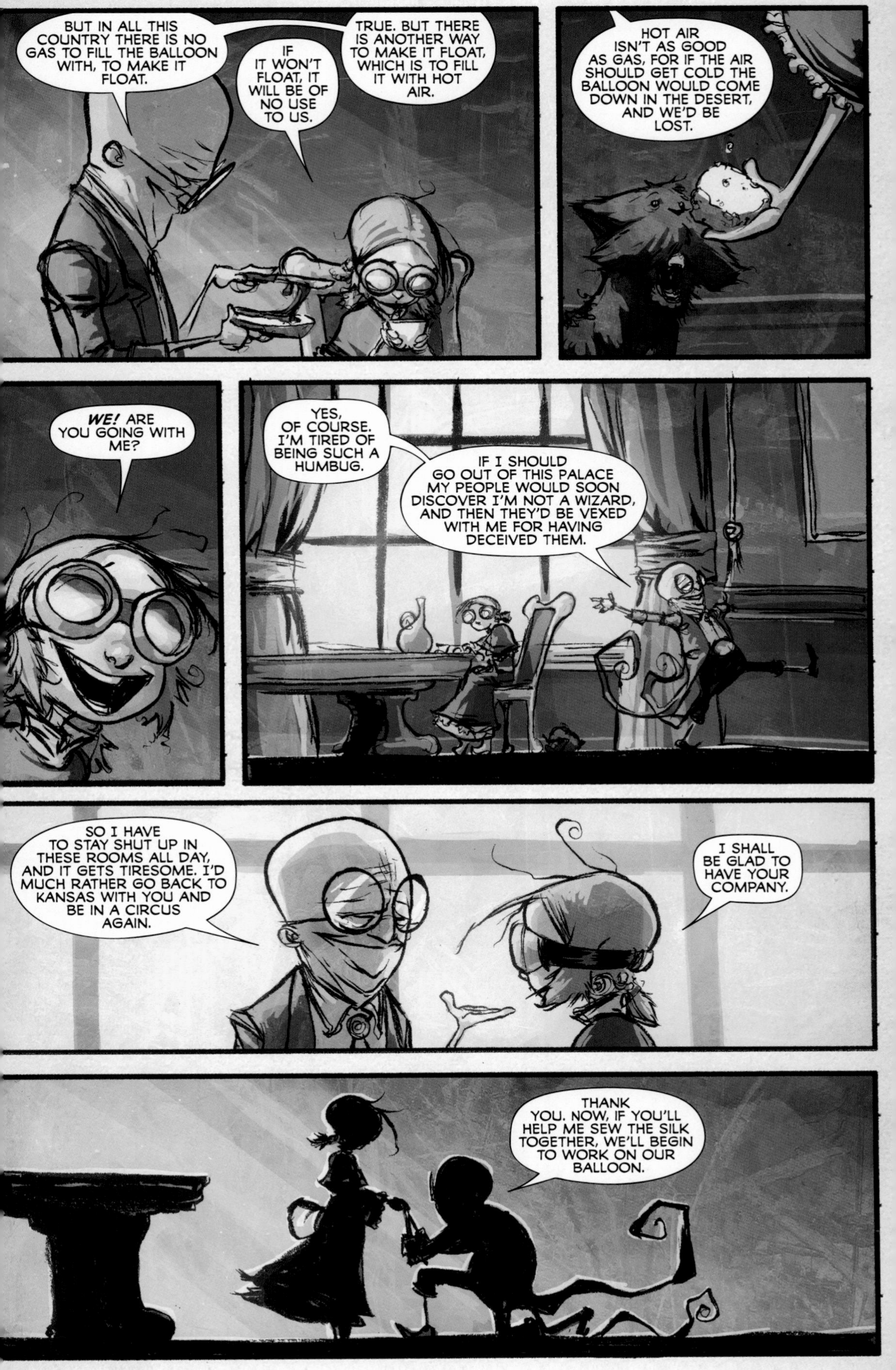
BUT IN ALL THIS COUNTRY THERE IS NO GAS TO FILL THE BALLOON WITH, TO MAKE IT FLOAT.
IF IT WON'T FLOAT, IT WILL BE OF NO USE TO US.
TRUE. BUT THERE IS ANOTHER WAY TO MAKE IT FLOAT, WHICH IS TO FILL IT WITH HOT AIR.
HOT AIR ISN'T AS GOOD AS GAS, FOR IF THE AIR SHOULD GET COLD THE BALLOON WOULD COME DOWN IN THE DESERT, AND WE'D BE LOST.
WE! ARE YOU GOING WITH ME?
YES, OF COURSE. I'M TIRED OF BEING SUCH A HUMBUG.
IF I SHOULD GO OUT OF THIS PALACE MY PEOPLE WOULD SOON DISCOVER I'M NOT A WIZARD, AND THEN THEY'D BE VEXED WITH ME FOR HAVING DECEIVED THEM.
SO I HAVE TO STAY SHUT UP IN THESE ROOMS ALL DAY, AND IT GETS TIRESOME. I'D MUCH RATHER GO BACK TO KANSAS WITH YOU AND BE IN A CIRCUS AGAIN.
I SHALL BE GLAD TO HAVE YOUR COMPANY.
THANK YOU. NOW, IF YOU'LL HELP ME SEW THE SILK TOGETHER, WE'LL BEGIN TO WORK ON OUR BALLOON.

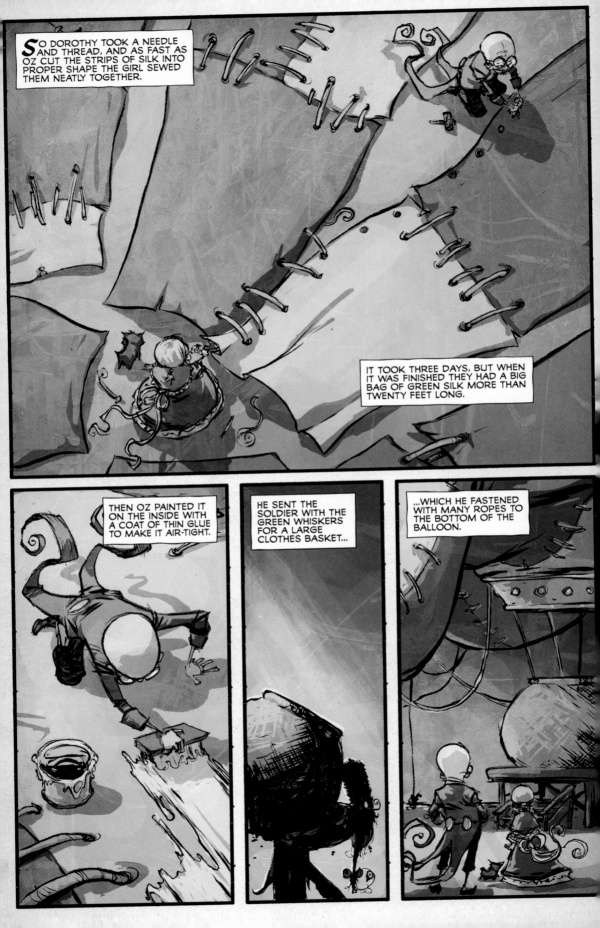

So Dorothy took a needle and thread, and as fast as Oz cut the strips of silk into proper shape the girl sewed them neatly together.

It took three days, but when it was finished they had a big bag of green silk more than twenty feet long.

Then Oz painted it on the inside with a coat of thin glue to make it air-tight.

He sent the soldier with the green whiskers for a large clothes basket...

...which he fastened with many ropes to the bottom of the balloon.

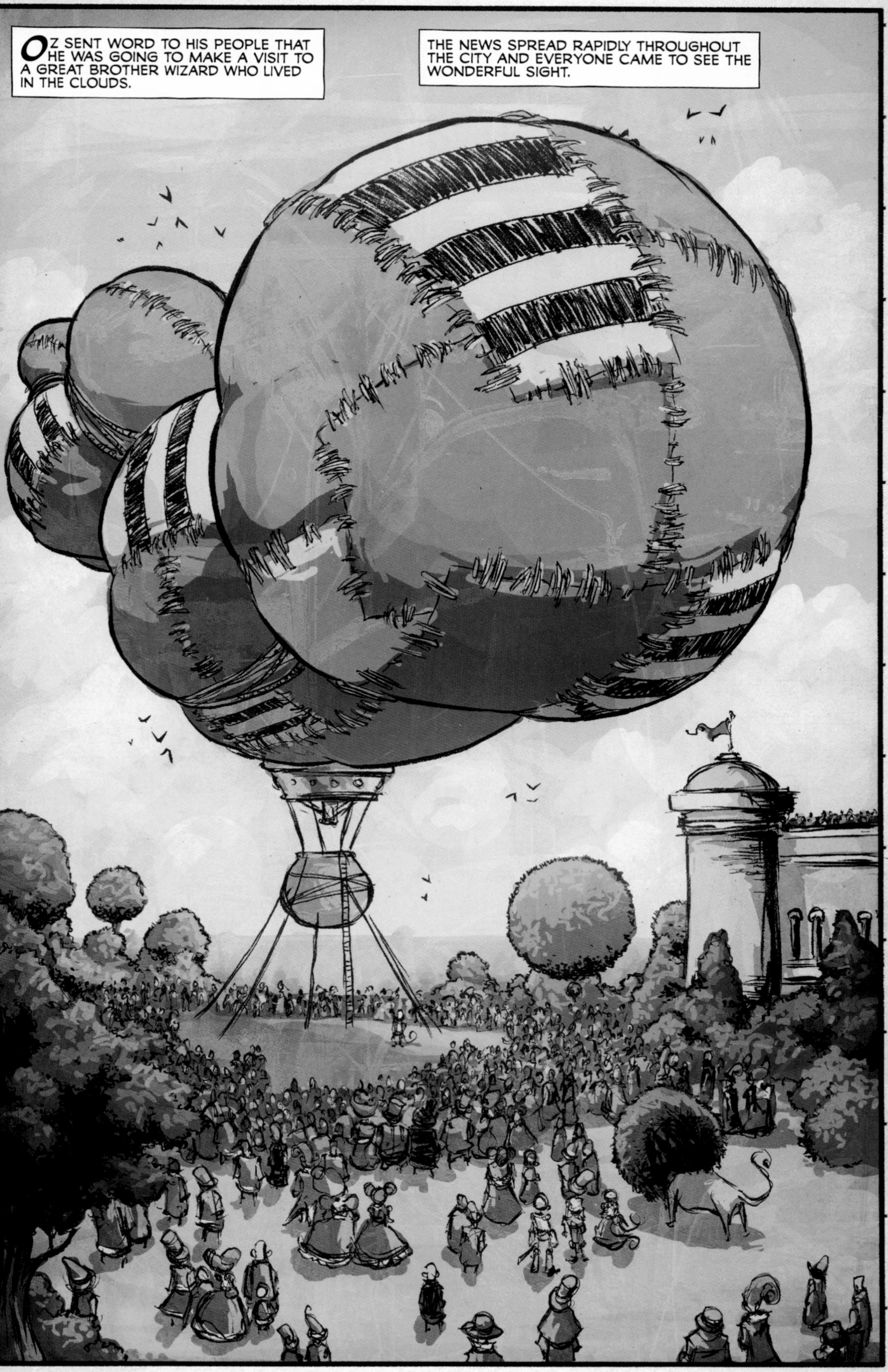
OZ SENT WORD TO HIS PEOPLE THAT HE WAS GOING TO MAKE A VISIT TO A GREAT BROTHER WIZARD WHO LIVED IN THE CLOUDS.
THE NEWS SPREAD RAPIDLY THROUGHOUT THE CITY AND EVERYONE CAME TO SEE THE WONDERFUL SIGHT.

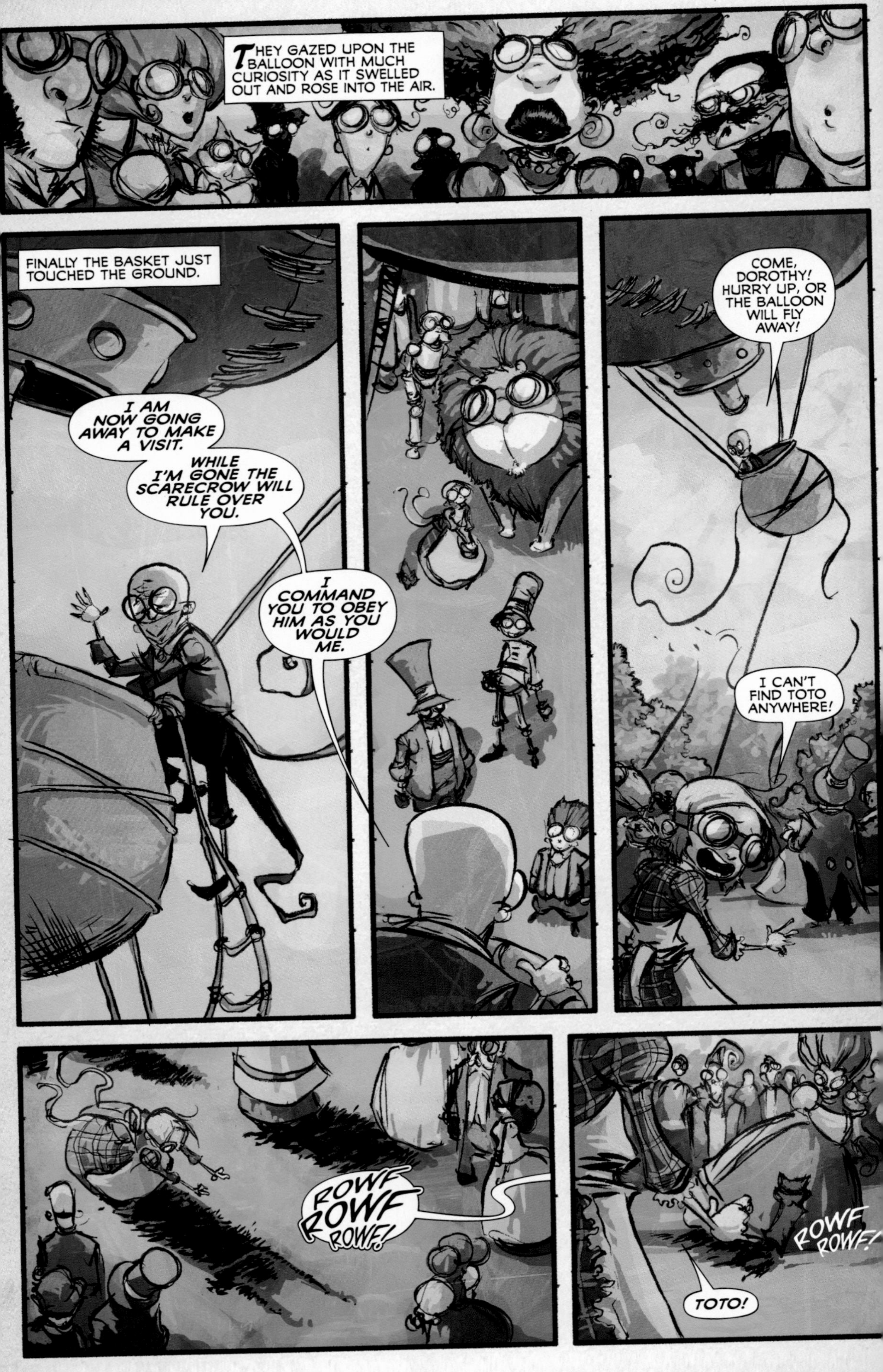
THEY GAZED UPON THE BALLOON WITH MUCH CURIOSITY AS IT SWELLED OUT AND ROSE INTO THE AIR.
FINALLY THE BASKET JUST TOUCHED THE GROUND.
I AM NOW GOING AWAY TO MAKE A VISIT.
WHILE I'M GONE THE SCARECROW WILL RULE OVER YOU.
I COMMAND YOU TO OBEY HIM AS YOU WOULD ME.
COME, DOROTHY! HURRY UP, OR THE BALLOON WILL FLY AWAY!
I CAN'T FIND TOTO ANYWHERE!
ROWF ROWF ROWF!
ROWF ROWF!
TOTO!

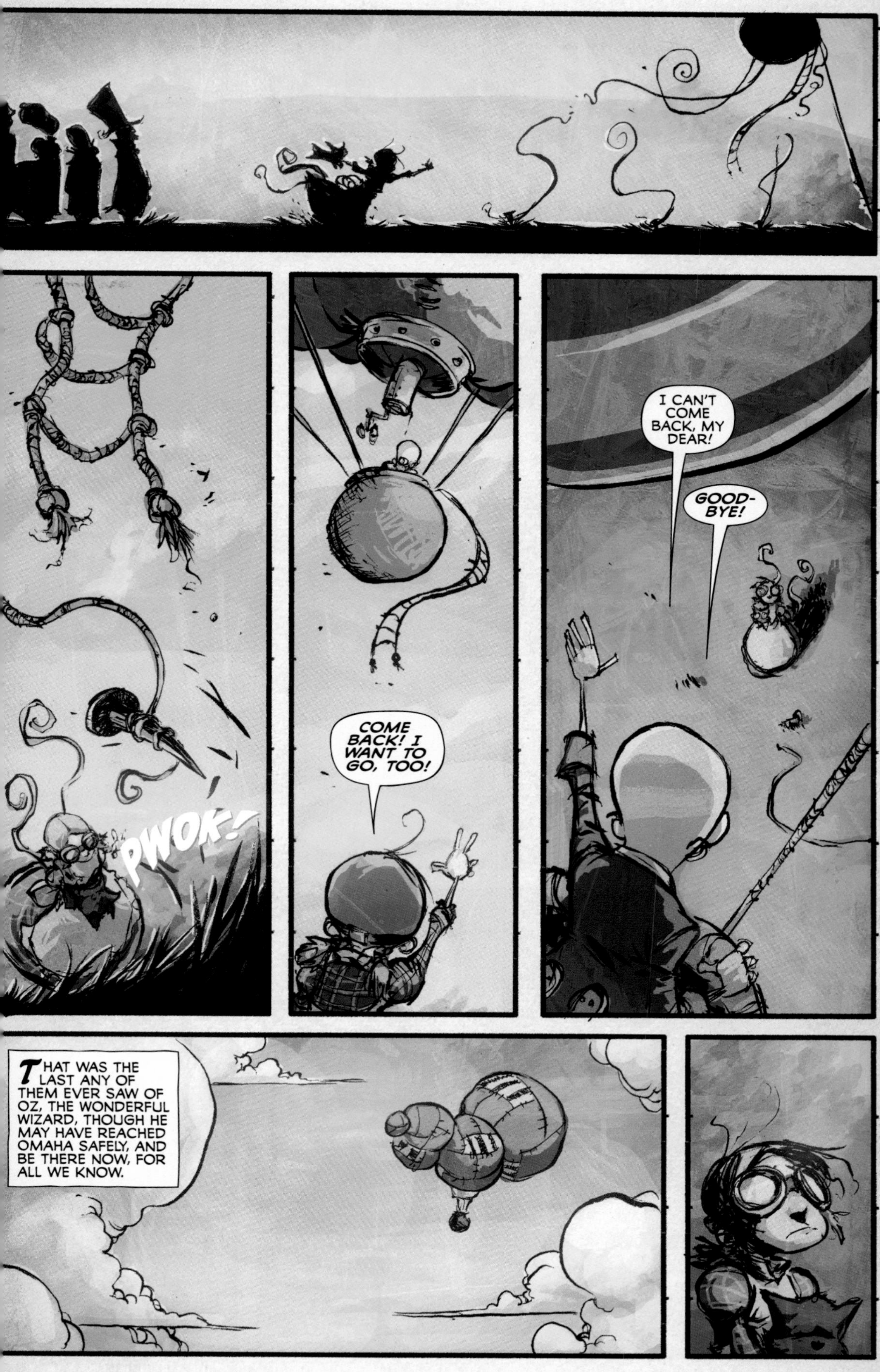
PWOK!
COME BACK! I WANT TO GO, TOO!
I CAN'T COME BACK, MY DEAR!
GOOD-BYE!
THAT WAS THE LAST ANY OF THEM EVER SAW OF OZ, THE WONDERFUL WIZARD, THOUGH HE MAY HAVE REACHED OMAHA SAFELY, AND BE THERE NOW, FOR ALL WE KNOW.

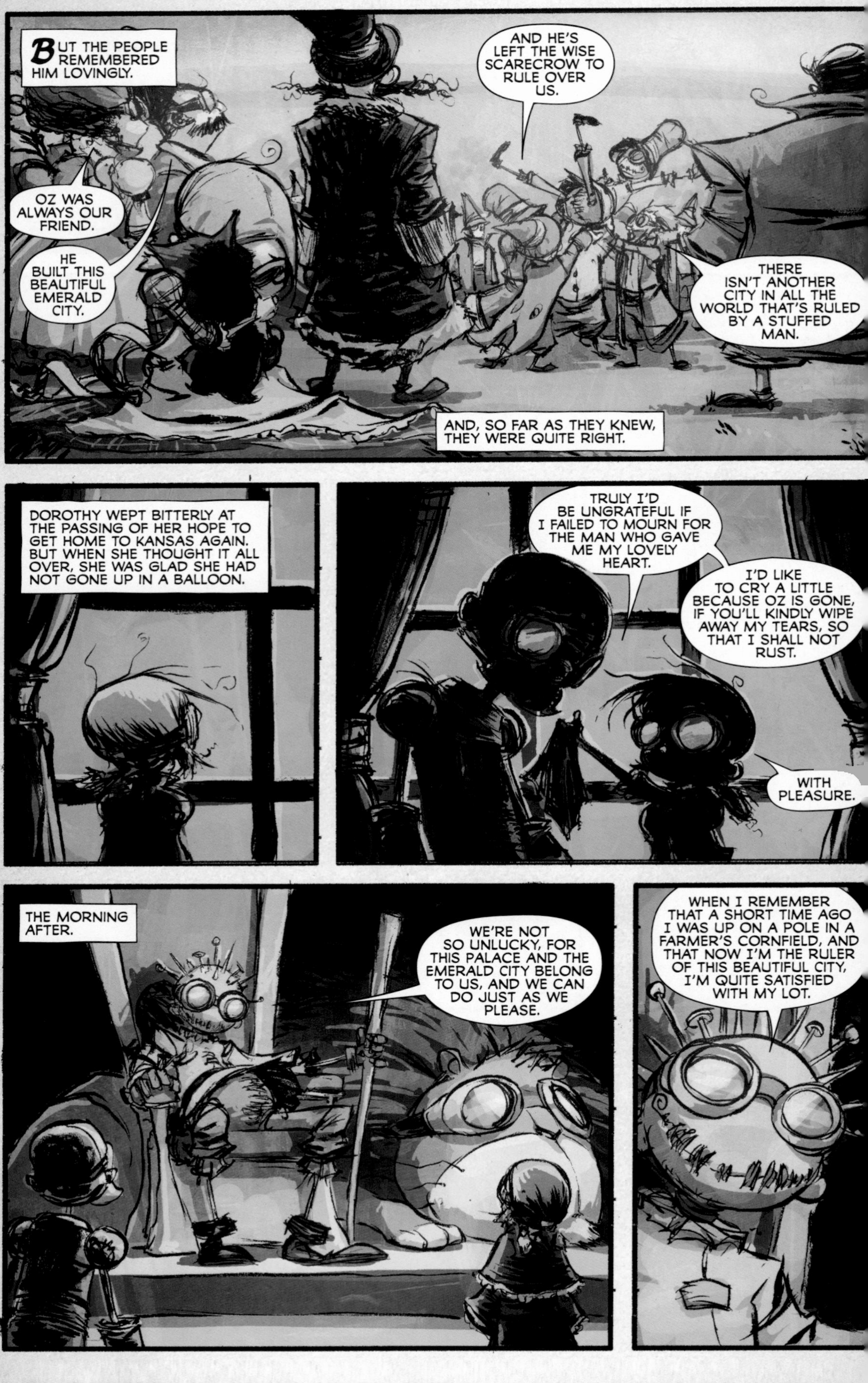
BUT THE PEOPLE REMEMBERED HIM LOVINGLY.
OZ WAS ALWAYS OUR FRIEND.
HE BUILT THIS BEAUTIFUL EMERALD CITY.
AND HE'S LEFT THE WISE SCARECROW TO RULE OVER US.
THERE ISN'T ANOTHER CITY IN ALL THE WORLD THAT'S RULED BY A STUFFED MAN.
AND, SO FAR AS THEY KNEW, THEY WERE QUITE RIGHT.
DOROTHY WEPT BITTERLY AT THE PASSING OF HER HOPE TO GET HOME TO KANSAS AGAIN. BUT WHEN SHE THOUGHT IT ALL OVER, SHE WAS GLAD SHE HAD NOT GONE UP IN A BALLOON.
TRULY I'D BE UNGRATEFUL IF I FAILED TO MOURN FOR THE MAN WHO GAVE ME MY LOVELY HEART.
I'D LIKE TO CRY A LITTLE BECAUSE OZ IS GONE, IF YOU'LL KINDLY WIPE AWAY MY TEARS, SO THAT I SHALL NOT RUST.
WITH PLEASURE.
THE MORNING AFTER.
WE'RE NOT SO UNLUCKY, FOR THIS PALACE AND THE EMERALD CITY BELONG TO US, AND WE CAN DO JUST AS WE PLEASE.
WHEN I REMEMBER THAT A SHORT TIME AGO I WAS UP ON A POLE IN A FARMER'S CORNFIELD, AND THAT NOW I'M THE RULER OF THIS BEAUTIFUL CITY, I'M QUITE SATISFIED WITH MY LOT.

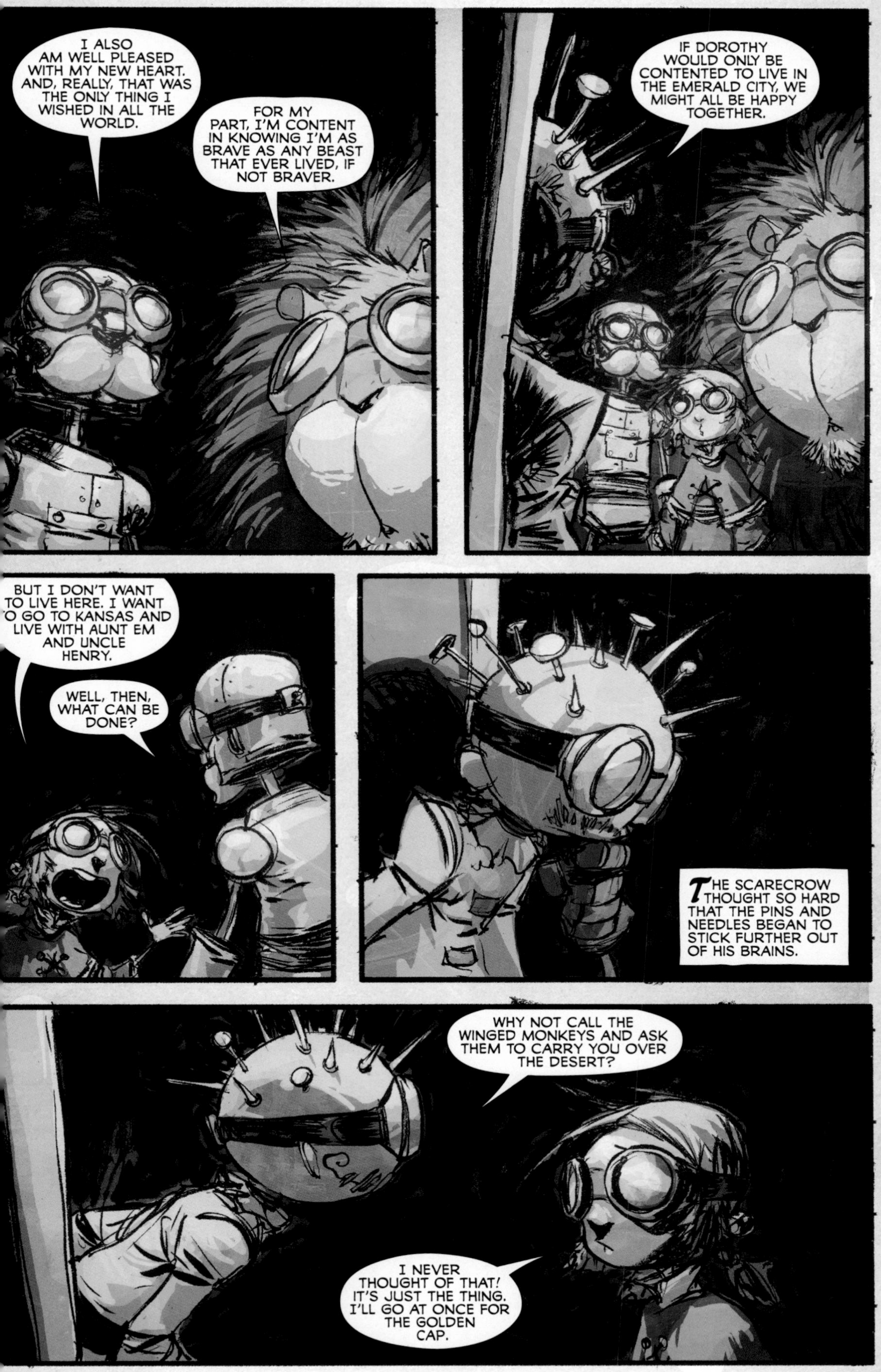
I ALSO AM WELL PLEASED WITH MY NEW HEART. AND, REALLY, THAT WAS THE ONLY THING I WISHED IN ALL THE WORLD.
FOR MY PART, I'M CONTENT IN KNOWING I'M AS BRAVE AS ANY BEAST THAT EVER LIVED, IF NOT BRAVER.
IF DOROTHY WOULD ONLY BE CONTENTED TO LIVE IN THE EMERALD CITY, WE MIGHT ALL BE HAPPY TOGETHER.
BUT I DON'T WANT TO LIVE HERE. I WANT TO GO TO KANSAS AND LIVE WITH AUNT EM AND UNCLE HENRY.
WELL, THEN, WHAT CAN BE DONE?
THE SCARECROW THOUGHT SO HARD THAT THE PINS AND NEEDLES BEGAN TO STICK FURTHER OUT OF HIS BRAINS.
WHY NOT CALL THE WINGED MONKEYS AND ASK THEM TO CARRY YOU OVER THE DESERT?
I NEVER THOUGHT OF THAT! IT'S JUST THE THING. I'LL GO AT ONCE FOR THE GOLDEN CAP.

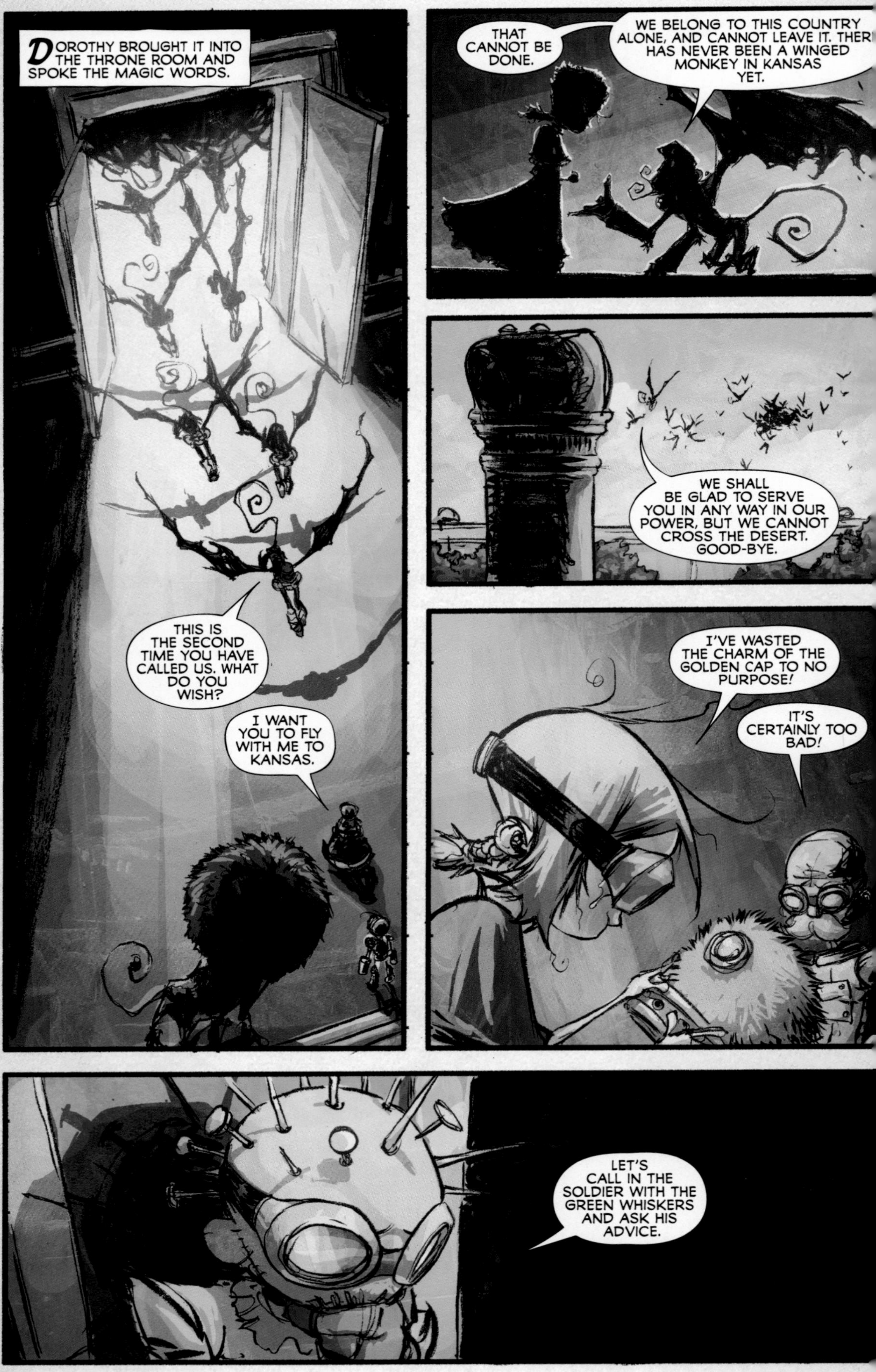
DOROTHY BROUGHT IT INTO THE THRONE ROOM AND SPOKE THE MAGIC WORDS.
THIS IS THE SECOND TIME YOU HAVE CALLED US. WHAT DO YOU WISH?
I WANT YOU TO FLY WITH ME TO KANSAS.
WE BELONG TO THIS COUNTRY ALONE, AND CANNOT LEAVE IT. THER HAS NEVER BEEN A WINGED MONKEY IN KANSAS YET.
THAT CANNOT BE DONE.
WE SHALL BE GLAD TO SERVE YOU IN ANY WAY IN OUR POWER, BUT WE CANNOT CROSS THE DESERT. GOOD-BYE.
I'VE WASTED THE CHARM OF THE GOLDEN CAP TO NO PURPOSE!
IT'S CERTAINLY TOO BAD!
LET'S CALL IN THE SOLDIER WITH THE GREEN WHISKERS AND ASK HIS ADVICE.

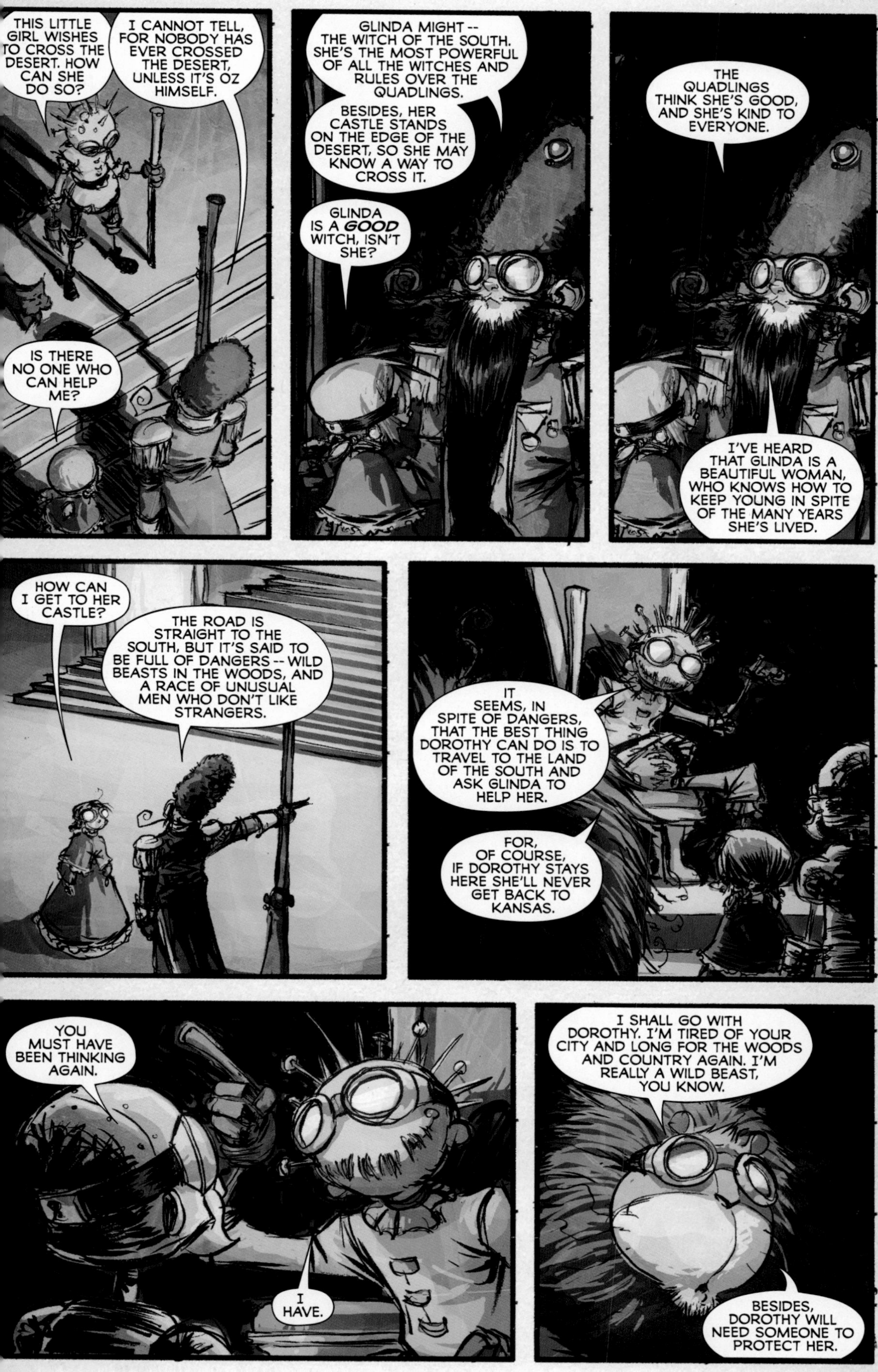
THIS LITTLE GIRL WISHES TO CROSS THE DESERT. HOW CAN SHE DO SO?
I CANNOT TELL, FOR NOBODY HAS EVER CROSSED THE DESERT, UNLESS IT'S OZ HIMSELF.
IS THERE NO ONE WHO CAN HELP ME?
GLINDA MIGHT -- THE WITCH OF THE SOUTH. SHE'S THE MOST POWERFUL OF ALL THE WITCHES AND RULES OVER THE QUADLINGS.
BESIDES, HER CASTLE STANDS ON THE EDGE OF THE DESERT, SO SHE MAY KNOW A WAY TO CROSS IT.
GLINDA IS A GOOD WITCH, ISN'T SHE?
THE QUADLINGS THINK SHE'S GOOD, AND SHE'S KIND TO EVERYONE.
I'VE HEARD THAT GLINDA IS A BEAUTIFUL WOMAN, WHO KNOWS HOW TO KEEP YOUNG IN SPITE OF THE MANY YEARS SHE'S LIVED.
HOW CAN I GET TO HER CASTLE?
THE ROAD IS STRAIGHT TO THE SOUTH, BUT IT'S SAID TO BE FULL OF DANGERS -- WILD BEASTS IN THE WOODS, AND A RACE OF UNUSUAL MEN WHO DON'T LIKE STRANGERS.
IT SEEMS, IN SPITE OF DANGERS, THAT THE BEST THING DOROTHY CAN DO IS TO TRAVEL TO THE LAND OF THE SOUTH AND ASK GLINDA TO HELP HER.
FOR, OF COURSE, IF DOROTHY STAYS HERE SHE'LL NEVER GET BACK TO KANSAS.
YOU MUST HAVE BEEN THINKING AGAIN.
I HAVE.
I SHALL GO WITH DOROTHY. I'M TIRED OF YOUR CITY AND LONG FOR THE WOODS AND COUNTRY AGAIN. I'M REALLY A WILD BEAST, YOU KNOW.
BESIDES, DOROTHY WILL NEED SOMEONE TO PROTECT HER.

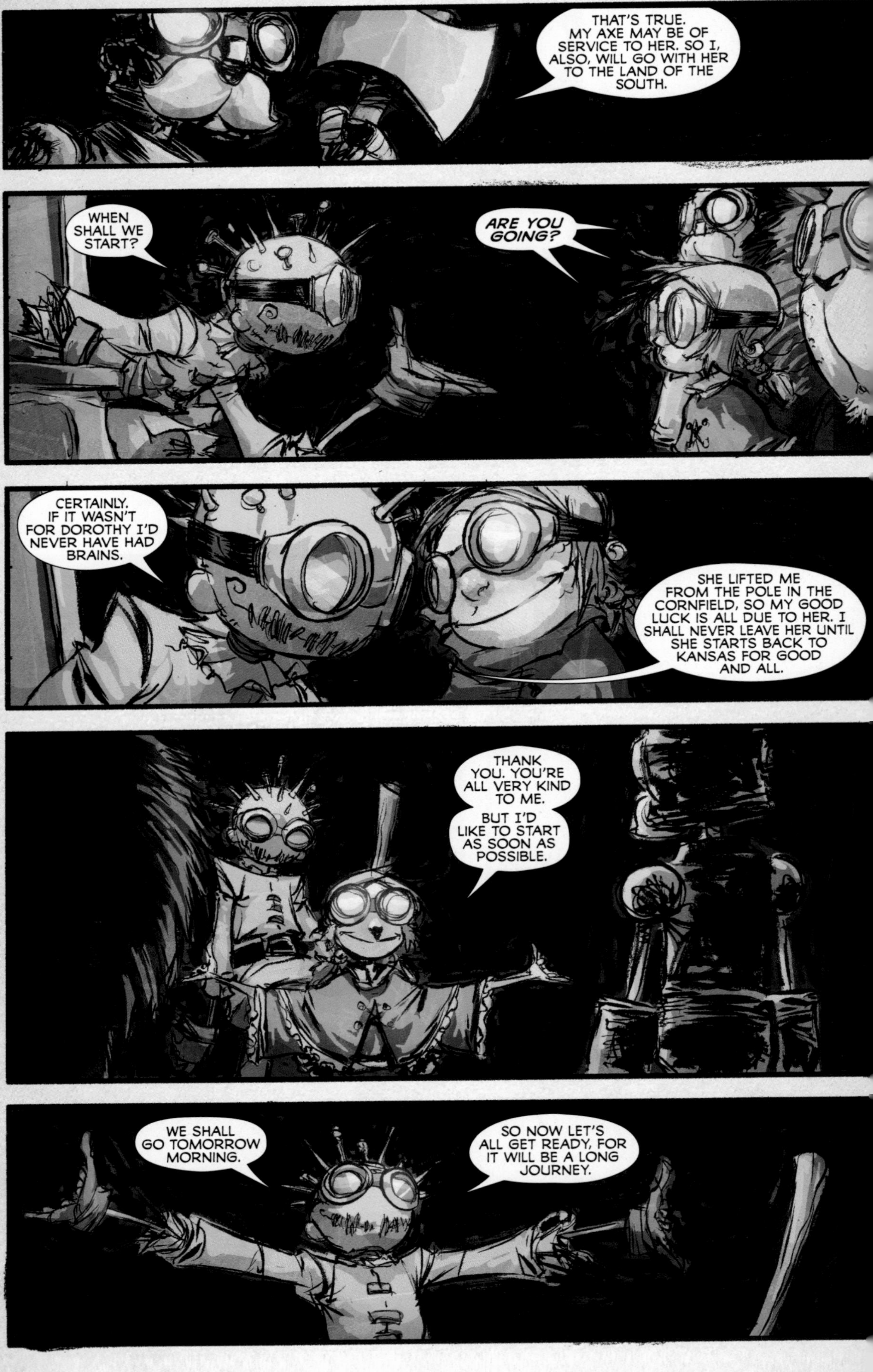
THAT'S TRUE. MY AXE MAY BE OF SERVICE TO HER. SO I, ALSO, WILL GO WITH HER TO THE LAND OF THE SOUTH.
WHEN SHALL WE START?
ARE YOU GOING?
CERTAINLY. IF IT WASN'T FOR DOROTHY I'D NEVER HAVE HAD BRAINS.
SHE LIFTED ME FROM THE POLE IN THE CORNFIELD, SO MY GOOD LUCK IS ALL DUE TO HER. I SHALL NEVER LEAVE HER UNTIL SHE STARTS BACK TO KANSAS FOR GOOD AND ALL.
THANK YOU. YOU'RE ALL VERY KIND TO ME.
BUT I'D LIKE TO START AS SOON AS POSSIBLE.
WE SHALL GO TOMORROW MORNING.
SO NOW LET'S ALL GET READY, FOR IT WILL BE A LONG JOURNEY.

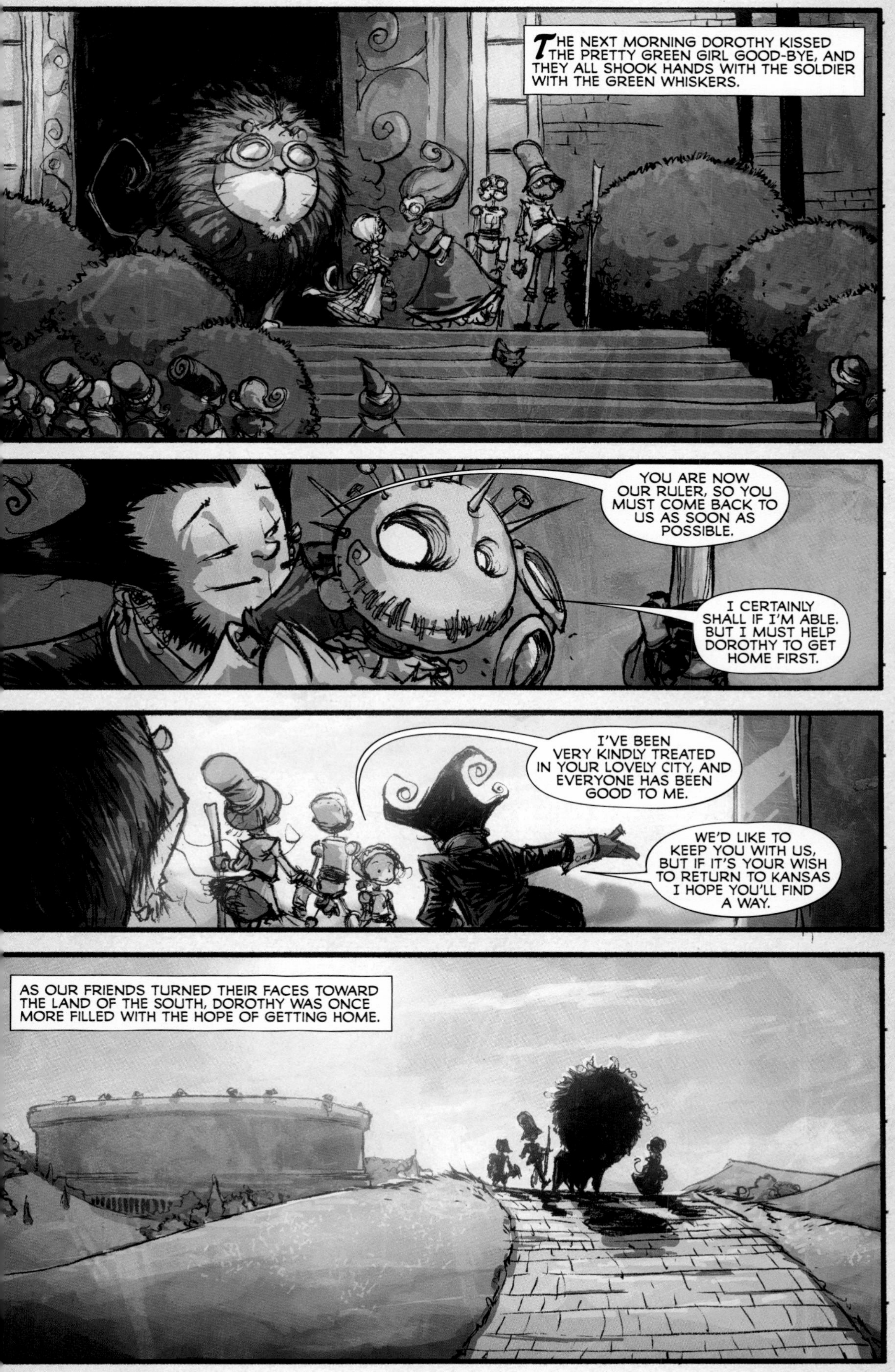
THE NEXT MORNING DOROTHY KISSED THE PRETTY GREEN GIRL GOOD-BYE, AND THEY ALL SHOOK HANDS WITH THE SOLDIER WITH THE GREEN WHISKERS.
YOU ARE NOW OUR RULER, SO YOU MUST COME BACK TO US AS SOON AS POSSIBLE.
I CERTAINLY SHALL IF I'M ABLE. BUT I MUST HELP DOROTHY TO GET HOME FIRST.
I'VE BEEN VERY KINDLY TREATED IN YOUR LOVELY CITY, AND EVERYONE HAS BEEN GOOD TO ME.
WE'D LIKE TO KEEP YOU WITH US, BUT IF IT'S YOUR WISH TO RETURN TO KANSAS I HOPE YOU'LL FIND A WAY.
AS OUR FRIENDS TURNED THEIR FACES TOWARD THE LAND OF THE SOUTH, DOROTHY WAS ONCE MORE FILLED WITH THE HOPE OF GETTING HOME.

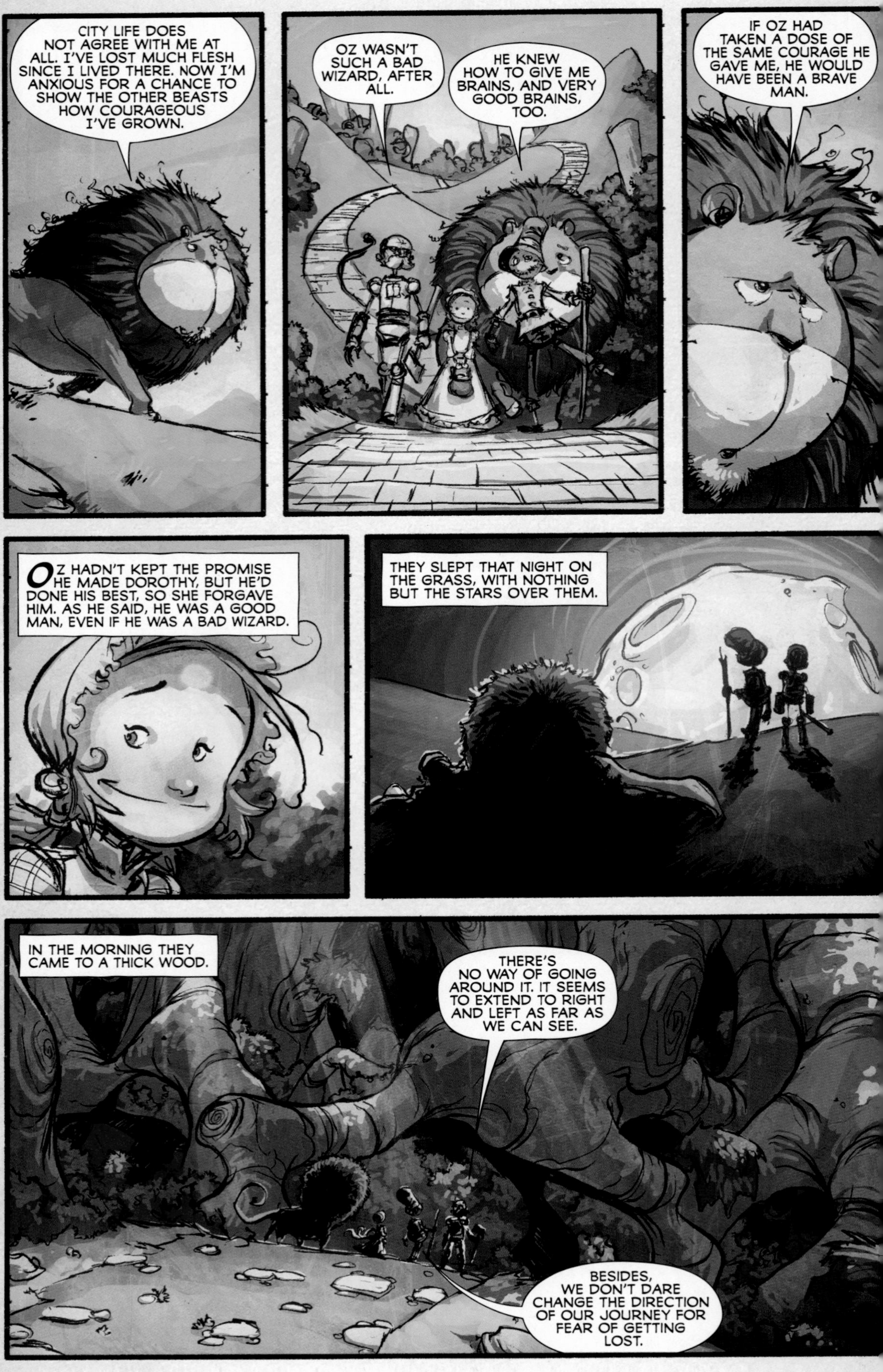
CITY LIFE DOES NOT AGREE WITH ME AT ALL. I'VE LOST MUCH FLESH SINCE I LIVED THERE. NOW I'M ANXIOUS FOR A CHANCE TO SHOW THE OTHER BEASTS HOW COURAGEOUS I'VE GROWN.
OZ WASN'T SUCH A BAD WIZARD, AFTER ALL.
HE KNEW HOW TO GIVE ME BRAINS, AND VERY GOOD BRAINS, TOO.
IF OZ HAD TAKEN A DOSE OF THE SAME COURAGE HE GAVE ME, HE WOULD HAVE BEEN A BRAVE MAN.
OZ HADN'T KEPT THE PROMISE HE MADE DOROTHY, BUT HE'D DONE HIS BEST, SO SHE FORGAVE HIM. AS HE SAID, HE WAS A GOOD MAN, EVEN IF HE WAS A BAD WIZARD.
THEY SLEPT THAT NIGHT ON THE GRASS, WITH NOTHING BUT THE STARS OVER THEM.
IN THE MORNING THEY CAME TO A THICK WOOD.
THERE'S NO WAY OF GOING AROUND IT. IT SEEMS TO EXTEND TO RIGHT AND LEFT AS FAR AS WE CAN SEE.
BESIDES, WE DON'T DARE CHANGE THE DIRECTION OF OUR JOURNEY FOR FEAR OF GETTING LOST.

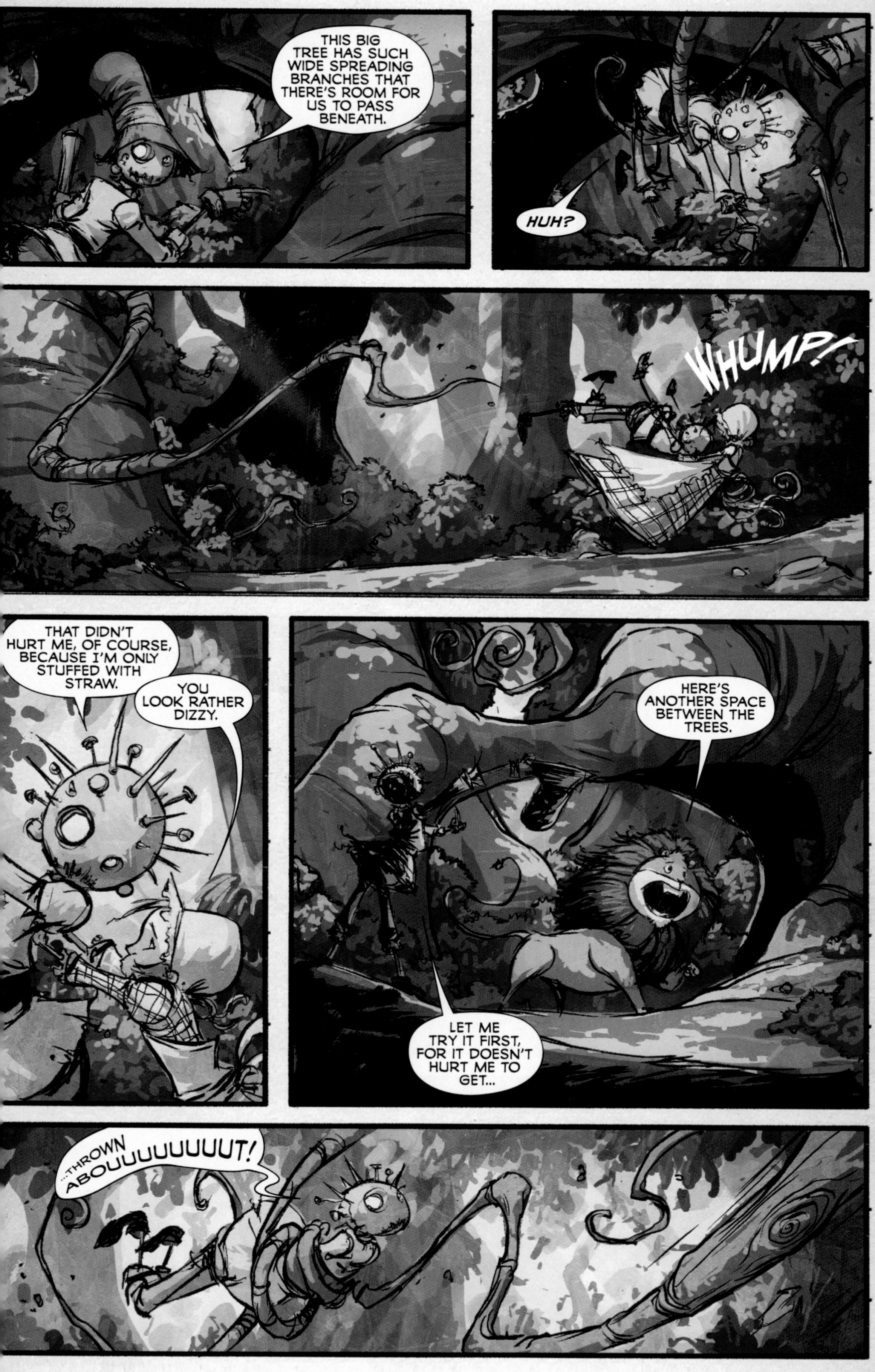
THIS BIG TREE HAS SUCH WIDE SPREADING BRANCHES THAT THERE'S ROOM FOR US TO PASS BENEATH.
HUH?
WHUMP!
THAT DIDN'T HURT ME, OF COURSE, BECAUSE I'M ONLY STUFFED WITH STRAW.
YOU LOOK RATHER DIZZY.
HERE'S ANOTHER SPACE BETWEEN THE TREES.
LET ME TRY IT FIRST, FOR IT DOESN'T HURT ME TO GET...
...THROWN ABOUUUUUUUUUT!

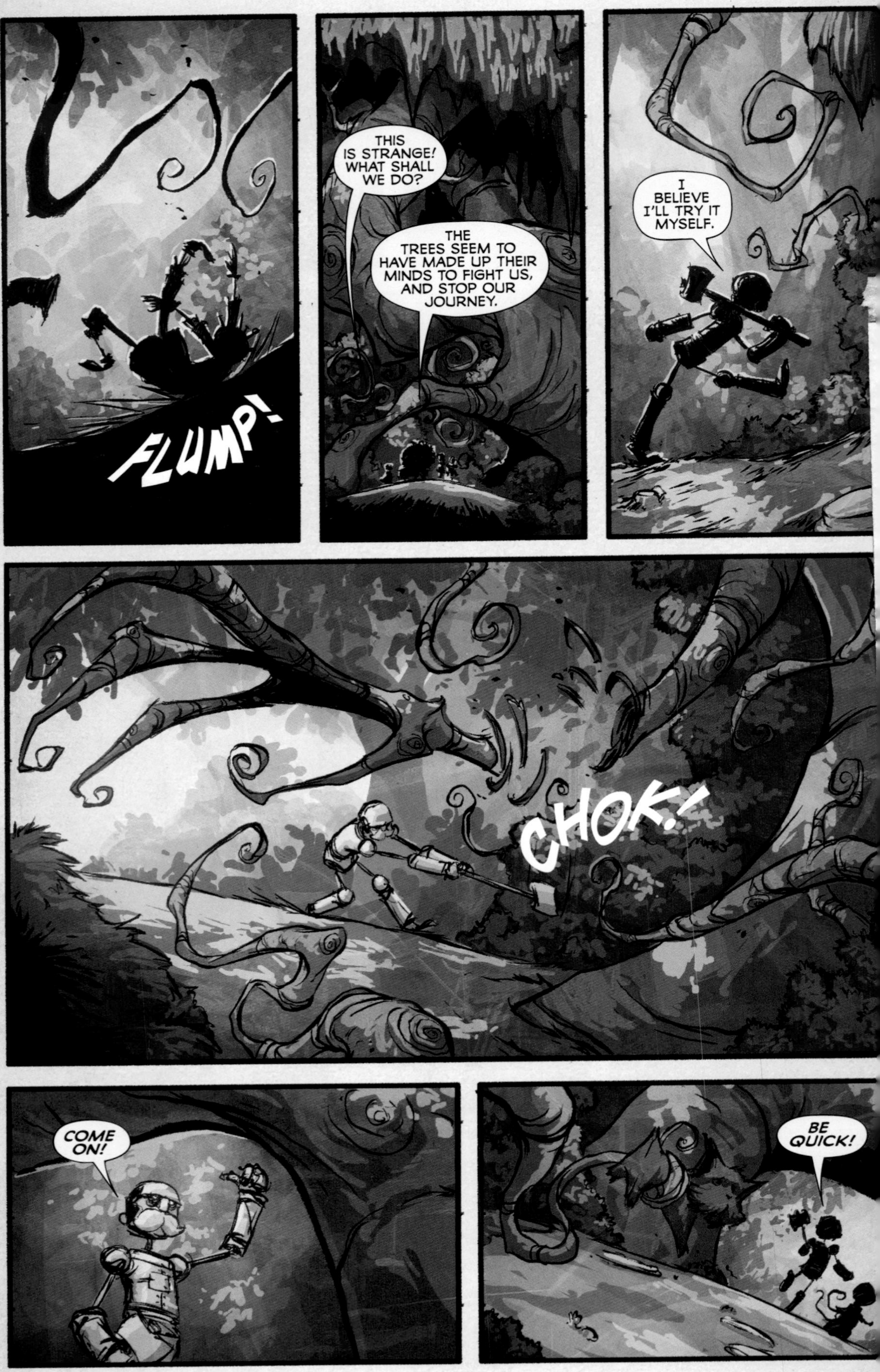
FLUMP!
THIS IS STRANGE! WHAT SHALL WE DO?
THE TREES SEEM TO HAVE MADE UP THEIR MINDS TO FIGHT US, AND STOP OUR JOURNEY.
I BELIEVE I'LL TRY IT MYSELF.
CHOK!
COME ON!
BE QUICK!

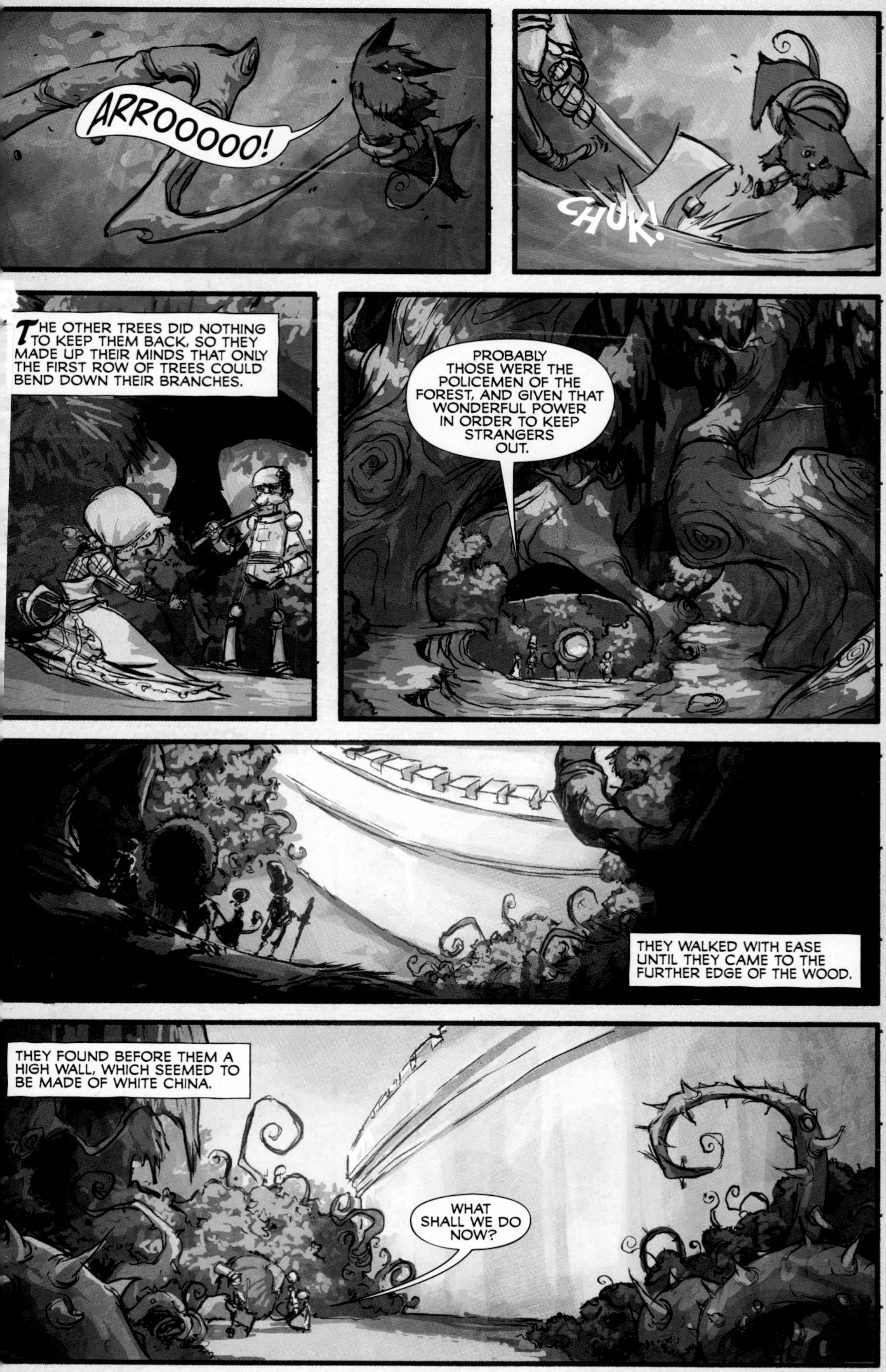
ARROOOOO!
CHUK!
THE OTHER TREES DID NOTHING TO KEEP THEM BACK, SO THEY MADE UP THEIR MINDS THAT ONLY THE FIRST ROW OF TREES COULD BEND DOWN THEIR BRANCHES.
PROBABLY THOSE WERE THE POLICEMEN OF THE FOREST, AND GIVEN THAT WONDERFUL POWER IN ORDER TO KEEP STRANGERS OUT.
THEY WALKED WITH EASE UNTIL THEY CAME TO THE FURTHER EDGE OF THE WOOD.
THEY FOUND BEFORE THEM A HIGH WALL, WHICH SEEMED TO BE MADE OF WHITE CHINA.
WHAT SHALL WE DO NOW?

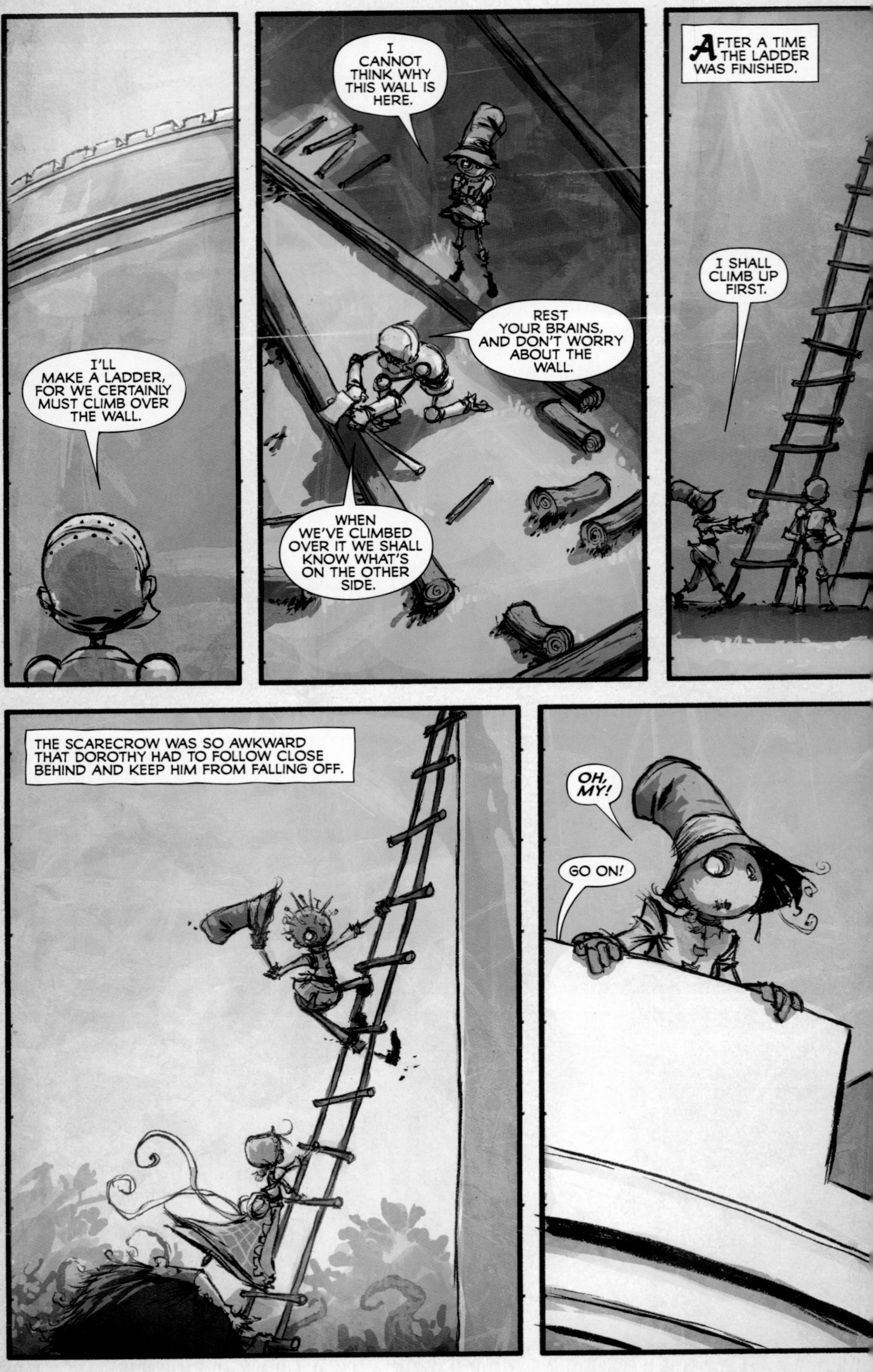
I'LL MAKE A LADDER, FOR WE CERTAINLY MUST CLIMB OVER THE WALL.
I CANNOT THINK WHY THIS WALL IS HERE.
REST YOUR BRAINS, AND DON'T WORRY ABOUT THE WALL.
WHEN WE'VE CLIMBED OVER IT WE SHALL KNOW WHAT'S ON THE OTHER SIDE.
AFTER A TIME THE LADDER WAS FINISHED.
I SHALL CLIMB UP FIRST.
THE SCARECROW WAS SO AWKWARD THAT DOROTHY HAD TO FOLLOW CLOSE BEHIND AND KEEP HIM FROM FALLING OFF.
OH, MY!
GO ON!